SHIKARI SHAMBU
TO THE RESCUE

"WHO ME?"

Conservationist, animal lover, wildlife expert, and your general firefighter for all problems—Shikari Shambu is known by all these names. But our man himself would rather snooze quietly in a corner than put one toe outside the house. But trouble always finds its way to Shikari Shambu and what follows is a maddening, hilarious adventure that will make you laugh and fall in love with this endearing shikari.

Created by former *Tinkle* editor, Luis Fernandes, and brought to life by V. B. Halbe, Shikari Shambu is one of the most popular characters in the *Tinkle* stable. Over 30+ years, he has had many adventures and run-ins with the wildest and most exotic of animals, birds, insects, plants, and, occasionally, humans. Illustrated by Savio Mascarenhas since 1998, Shambu has only gone from funny to funnier.

Readers Speak:

"Shikari Shambu rocks! Please never even think of discontinuing it." – **Riddhi Devadiga,** via email

"I request you to publish Shikari Shambu every month, as he is one of my favourite toons!" – **Ashwini Ballal,** Aurangabad

"Shikari Shambu never fails to mesmerize me." – **Neha Binwal,** via email

"I am in love with all the Tinkle toons, especially Shikari Shambu." – **Harish Menon,** via email

"I like Shikari Shambu because his stories are informative." – **Pratik Gadgil,** Mumbai

"Shikari Shambu stories are just amazing! Each story follows a different theme. It's totally cool along with the eye-boggling illustrations of Savio." – **Vilas M.,** via email

"I am happy to see Savio still illustrating Shikari Shambu in his trademark style." – **Unmesh Damle,** via email

"I am afraid of animals and so my uncle always calls me Shikari Shambu!" – **Hitarth Vaishnav,** via email

The Legend of Shikari Shambu — 3
Shikari Shambu The Cowboy — 9
Circus! Circus! — 14
DIY: Bird Bath — 19
The Haunted House — 20
Sleepy Hero — 26
Colour Me Bright! — 31
To Catch a Croc — 32
Best Places to Take a Nap — 42
Early Birds — 43
The Swamp Monster — 50
Q&A with Shikari Shambu — 56
Thepla! — 57
Quiz Time! — 64
To Catch a Killer — 65

"I MADE THE MISTAKE OF TAKING TO MY HEELS...

"THE CANINES CAME BOUNDING AFTER ME...

* Bushes of short woody plants with tough, rigid, interlacing branches.

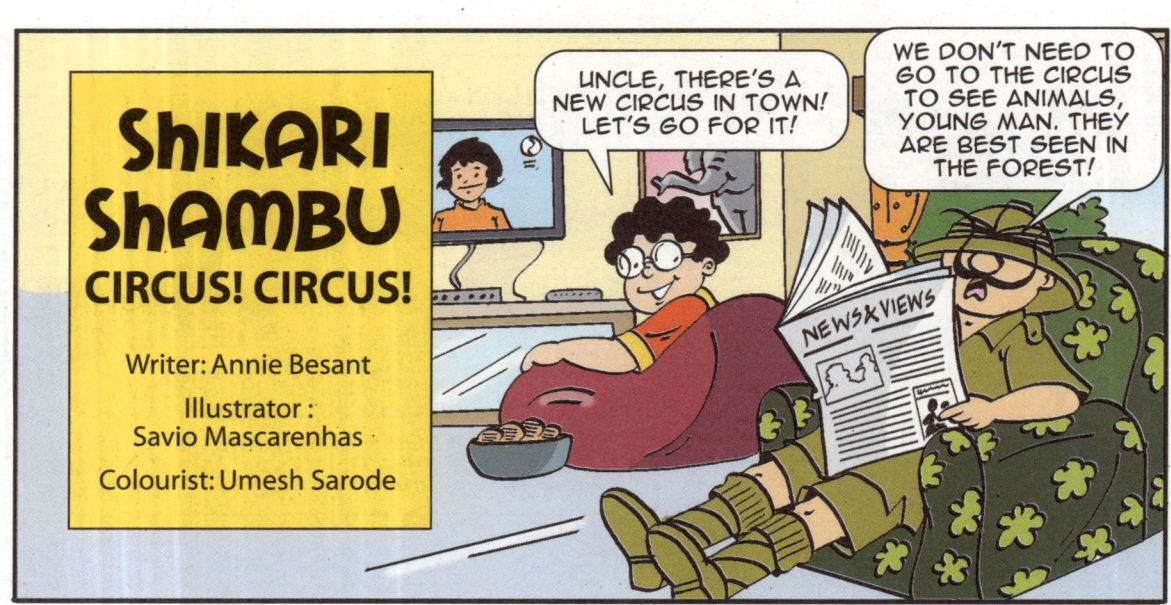

DIY: Bird Bath

One of the biggest problems that our birds face today is finding clean water to drink or have a cool bath in. So I searched through my house, looking for things that I could use as a bird bath for my friends. And guess what I found:

A Plate: Pretty easy to find, right? Especially, if you're a food lover like me, you'll always know where the plates are kept. So find a nice, clean one, put it outside on the window grille or any other steady platform, and fill the plate with water. That's it, you're done!

A Big Bowl: Ah, yes. Now, this one is nifty too. Works the same way as the plate. But with the bowl, you can also hang it outside your window to make a swinging bird bath. All you have to do is—tie a rope around the bowl, and then, with 2-3 other ropes tie each rope to the rope tied around the bowl, and then knot them together at the centre to hang it.

A Lunch Box: If you're buying a new lunch box, then don't throw away your old lunch box if it is big and deep. Just clean it up, place it outside your window, fill it with water, and watch the birds fly to your nest.

A Tray: A tray is a good idea because it has got a flat bottom, so there's no chance of the tray wobbling or tripping. A shallow surface also works for birds because they tend to walk in water and spray the water all over them. So the tray definitely serves well as a bird bath!

A Plant Pot: Did you think I was only searching in the kitchen for food, I mean, bird bath tools? He-he. No, I looked around in my garden and I found an empty pot, which is surprising because I grow lots of plants. Anyway, for this empty pot, I sealed the hole in its bottom and poured clean water in.

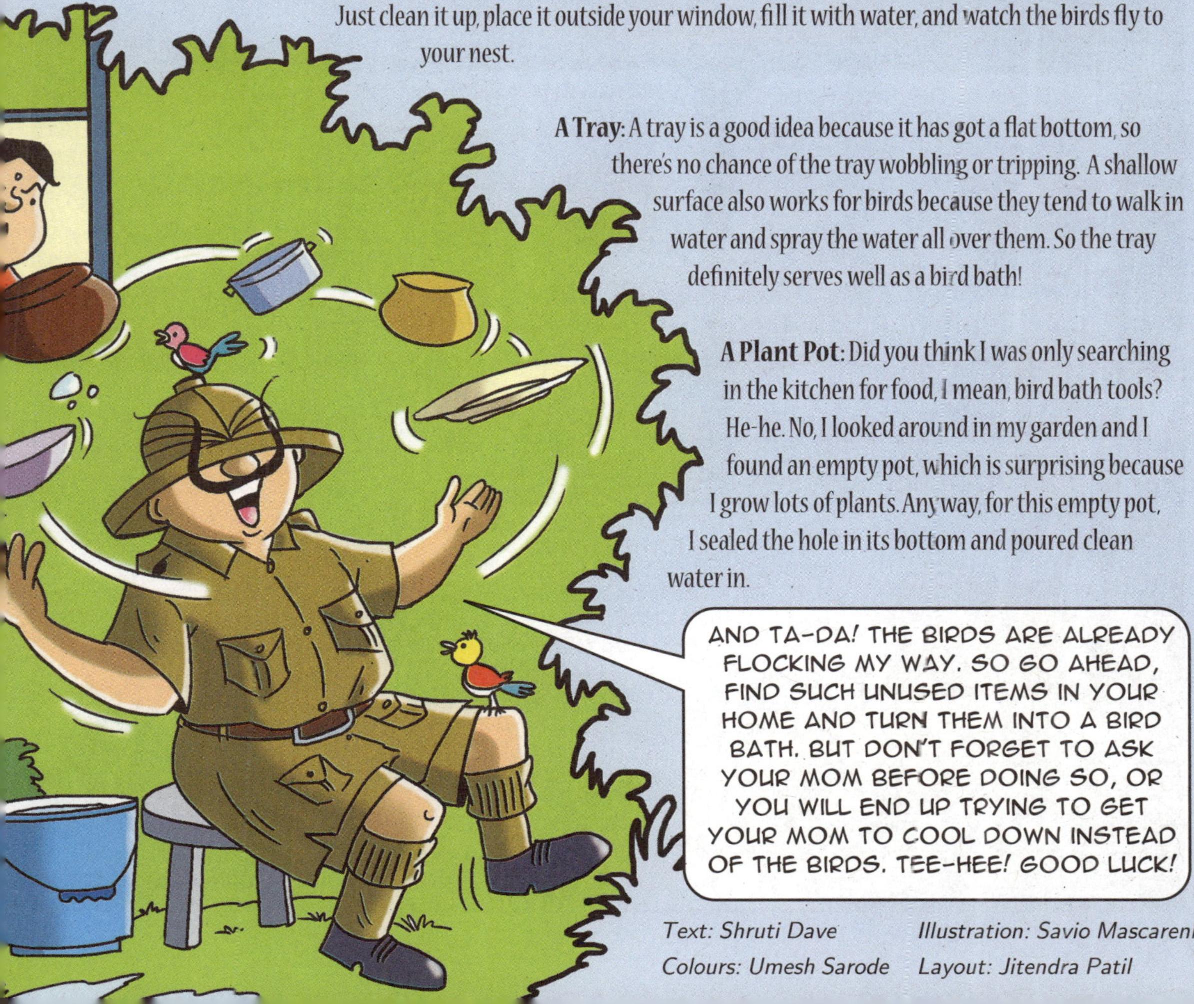

AND TA-DA! THE BIRDS ARE ALREADY FLOCKING MY WAY. SO GO AHEAD, FIND SUCH UNUSED ITEMS IN YOUR HOME AND TURN THEM INTO A BIRD BATH. BUT DON'T FORGET TO ASK YOUR MOM BEFORE DOING SO, OR YOU WILL END UP TRYING TO GET YOUR MOM TO COOL DOWN INSTEAD OF THE BIRDS. TEE-HEE! GOOD LUCK!

Text: Shruti Dave Illustration: Savio Mascarenhas
Colours: Umesh Sarode Layout: Jitendra Patil

Shikari Shambu in 'The Haunted House'

Writer: Anomita Guha
Illustrator: Savio Mascarenhas
Colourist: Umesh Sarode

COLOUR ME BRIGHT!

SUBSCRIBE NOW!

TINKLE MAGAZINE		TINKLE DIGEST		TINKLE COMBO MAGAZINE + DIGEST	
FREE* ACK DVD *with 2 year subscription		FREE ACK DVD		FREE ACK DVD	
1 yr subscription	2 yr subscription	1 yr subscription	2 yr subscription	1 yr subscription	2 yr subscription
Pay only ₹480 ₹380!	Pay only ₹960 ₹750!	Pay only ₹720 ₹580!	Pay only ₹1440 ₹1080!	Pay only ₹1200 ₹880!	Pay only ₹2400 ₹1680!

I would like a subscription for

TINKLE MAGAZINE ☐ 1 yr ☐ 2 yrs   TINKLE COMBO ☐ 1 yr ☐ 2 yrs   TINKLE DIGEST ☐ 1 yr ☐ 2 yrs

(Please tick the appropriate box)

YOUR DETAILS*

Name: .... Date of Birth: |__|__| / |__|__| / |__|__|__|__|

Address: ....

.... City: .... Pin: |__|__|__|__|__|__| State: ....

School: .... Class: ....

Tel: .... Mobile: +91 - |__|__|__|__|__|__|__|__|__|__|

Email: .... Signature: ....

PAYMENT OPTIONS

☐ Cheque /DD:

Please enclose Cheque /DD no. |__|__|__|__|__|__| drawn in favour of 'ACK Media Direct Ltd.'

at .... (bank) for the amount .... ,

dated |__|__| / |__|__| / |__|__|__|__| and send it to: ACK Media Direct Ltd., 201 & 202, Sumer Plaza, 2nd Floor, Marol Maroshi Road, Andheri (East), Mumbai- 400 059.

☐ Pay Cash on Delivery: Pay cash on delivery of the first issue to the postman. (Additional charge of ₹50 applicable)

☐ Pay by money order: Pay by money order in favour of "ACK Media Direct Ltd."

☐ Online subscription: Please visit: www.amarchitrakatha.com

For any queries or further information: Email: customerservice@ack-media.com or Call: 022-40497417 / 31

BEST PLACES TO TAKE A NAP

Did you know that taking a nap during the day has several advantages? And no, I'm not making this up just because I love sleeping. Research says that napping improves your mood, mental alertness and creativity. Now from my vast experience in snoozing around, I've made a list of my favourite places to take a nap. Check it out—

Hammock

Ah... the gentle swaying of the hammock immediately puts me to sleep (not that I need much cajoling!). As I fall into the deep curve of the hammock, I fall into an equally deep sleep. ☺ And the best thing I like about the hammock is that it's where I like to stay the most—outdoors.

Bean Bag

Some times I'm so sleepy that I can barely keep my eyes open or even walk. At times like these, I love crashing on my bean bag. They provide the ultimate relaxation as they mould as per my sleeping position. What's more, bean bags are eco-friendly too since they're not made of wood. It's like a double scoop of ice-cream!

Pool Float

Whenever I find an empty, quiet pool, I dive straight into it with my floating bed. The constant rhythm of the water under your float will make you lose track of time, giving you hours of peaceful sleep. You only need to train yourself not too move around too much on the float, or you will be rudely awakened by a dunking. Me, I don't like too much physical movement as it is, so the pool float is a lovely place to float away to sweet dreams.

Grass

The chirps of the birds around you, the floating clouds above you and the cool grass tickling your feet... what better place to relax than on cool grass? Most of the times, I can't fall into deep sleep here because I get too fascinated by all the little creatures around me. Still, lying on grass is as refreshing as waking up after 10 hours of sleep.

Anywhere

Yeah, well, at the end of the day, as long as you manage to catch a few winks, everything is hunky-dory when and wherever you wake up. ☺ Right?

Text: Shruti Dave   Layout: Jitendra P

Shikari Shambu and the Swamp Monster

Inspired by a story sent by **Anuradha Chakrabortty**
Script: Rajani Thindiath
Illustrator and Colourist: Savio Mascarenhas

Q&A WITH SHIKARI SHAMBU, FRIEND OF ANIMALS

Text: Shruti Dave   Layout: Jitendra Patil

Hello, Shambu Sir. It is a pleasure to finally meet and talk to you.
Oh, no. The pleasure is all mine-nah (like Mynah). Ha ha ha!

Ha ha ha! JJ was right; you are funny. Anyway, Shambu Sir, you have dedicated your life to helping animals. Can you tell us why you chose this career path?
Uh, well. Frankly, I did not choose this life. This life chose me! You can know more about how my career kicked off in 'The Legend of Shikari Shambu' story. Besides that, we share our world with animals and it's only fair that we look after each other. Animals, birds, insects, all of them help our ecosystem, and we, in turn, should help and look after their well being.

Hmm. That is so true. Sir, can you tell us how we, in small ways or big, can help these animals?
That's a great question! Yes, there are many small steps you can take. Firstly, please minimize your use of plastic. The plastic bags that you use land up in garbage cans, from where cows, stray dogs, cats, and birds often eat. Obviously, this is harmful to their health.

Yes, definitely. Plastic not only harms our animal friends but also pollutes our environment.
Then, most importantly, take care of the animals around you, your home, your locality. Just as you decorate your room with your favourite colours and cartoons, create a happy and safe environment for your friends as well. Grow plants in your balcony, build bird baths and feeders, use eco-friendly ways to get rid off pests, don't litter, etc. These are some of the simple ways to make a happy home for animals. Also, if you see any animal or bird in need of help don't walk away. Call an adult or animal care centre for help.

Great piece of advice, Shambu Sir. I also think we should adopt more and more of our Indian stray dogs.
Yes, if you want a pet, why not give a nice home to our stray dogs? Adopting foreign animals and birds may not be a good idea as these foreign breeds may not be suited to the Indian climate. Nevertheless, if you have a pet, take utmost care of them. Play with them, give them your loving attention and feed them properly.

Thank you so much for your time, Shikari Shambu. I'm sure our readers will be encouraged by your words. Can you tell us a little about your future plans?
Oh, yes. I intend to check out the restaurant next door. I hear their aloo parathas are fabulous.

Ha ha ha! That's Shikari Shambu for you, folks. Until next time!

*Flatbread made with fenugreek leaves.

Quiz Time

I love all animals, birds, fishes, and insects. But there are some animals with whom I share some special traits. He-he! To find out which animals I'm talking about, take the quiz below:

1. Which is the sleepiest animal?
a. Koala   b. Sloth   c. Hippopotamus

2. Which animal eats the most in a day?
a. Seal   b. Elephant   c. Blue Whale

3. Which is the slowest animal in the world?
a. Snail   b. Tortoise   c. Three-toed sloth

4. Which insect helps the environment the most?
a. Honeybee   b. Beetle   c. Lady Bug

5. Which is the second most intelligent animal after humans?
a. Pigs   b. Dolphins   c. Chimpanzees

Answers:
1. Koala, it sleeps for up to 22 hours, out of 24 hours a day!
2. Blue Whale, it eats approximately 3,000 to 7,000 kilo of krill every day!
3. Three-toed sloth, its top speed is around 0.24 km/per hour!
4. Honeybee, it helps in the process of pollination and makes sweet, yummy honey!
5. Chimpanzees, they can solve many types of problems and even use sign language!

Text: Shruti Dave
Illustrations: Savio Mascarenhas